For Chet Pierce

VIKING
Published by the Penguin Group
Penguin Putnam Books for Young Readers, 345 Hudson Street,
New York, New York 10014, U.S.A.
Penguin Books Ltd, 27 Wrights Lane, London W8 5TZ, England
Penguin Books Australia Ltd, Ringwood, Victoria, Australia
Penguin Books Canada Ltd, 10 Alcorn Avenue, Toronto,
Ontario, Canada M4V 3B2
Penguin Books (N.Z.) Ltd, 182-190 Wairau Road,
Auckland 10, New Zealand

Penguin Books Ltd, Registered Offices: Harmondsworth,
Middlesex, England

First published in the United States of America by the
Macmillan Company, 1971
Published by Viking and Puffin Books,
members of Penguin Putnam Books for Young Readers, 1999

10 9 8 7 6 5 4 3 2 1

LIBRARY OF CONGRESS CATALOGING-IN-PUBLICATION DATA
Keats, Ezra Jack.
Apt. 3 / Ezra Jack Keats.
p.   cm.
Summary: On a rainy day two brothers try to discover who is
playing the harmonica they hear in their apartment building.
ISBN 0-670-88342-5 — ISBN 0-14-056507-8 (pbk.)
[1. Apartment houses—Fiction. 2. Brothers—Fiction.
3. Blind—Fiction. 4. Physically handicapped—Fiction.
5. City and town life—Fiction.] I. Title.
PZ7.K2253Ap 1999 [E]—dc21 98-41043 CIP AC

Printed in Hong Kong

EZRA
JACK
KEATS
APT. 3

VIKING

The rain fell steadily.
It beat against the windows,
softening the sounds of the city.
As Sam gazed out, he heard someone
in the building playing a harmonica.
It filled him with sad and lonely feelings—
like the rain outside.
He had heard that music before.
Each time it was different.
"Who's that playing?" Sam wondered.

Sam went into the hall and listened. No music.
His little brother Ben tagged along.
Sam listened at the door across the hall.
Crunch, crunch, crunch.
Crunch, crackle, crunch!
Someone—or something—turned the knob.

Out came Mr. Muntz,
crunching a mouthful
of potato chips.

They waited until he was gone.
There was one door left on their floor.
Through it came smells of cigarettes and cooking.
A family was arguing.
But no music.

They walked down to the floor below.
A dog was barking—real mean—in Apt. 9.
Next door a mother sang softly
to her crying baby.
At Apt. 7, not a sound.

Down another flight.
The hall light was broken.
At Apt. 6, there was a ball game on TV.
It sounded like a million people were in there cheering.
Apt. 5—loud, juicy snoring.
Ben bumped into an old, worn-out mattress.
"That snorer sure's enjoying his new one," Sam said.
Apt. 4—more yelling.

Finally, the ground floor.
The door of Apt. 1 opened.
"The super!" Sam whispered.
They hid under the stairs.
The super grumbled to himself
as he left the building and slammed the door.
"That guy hates everyone," said Ben.

Apt. 3 was quiet.
Just a container of milk outside the door.
They stopped in front of Apt. 2—Betsy's door.
Sam thought, "Maybe she'll come out
and I'll say hello to her."
He decided to hang around.
"Let's rest a little," he said.
They sat on the steps.

But no Betsy.
And no music.
"C'mon, let's go home," said Ben.

As they turned to go upstairs, Sam noticed
that the container of milk was gone!

He went over to take a good look.

The door was open a little.

He peeked in.

"WELL?" A sharp voice startled Sam.

"We didn't take the milk!" he blurted.

But the man was shouting, "O.K., nosy!

Have a good look!"

Sam could make out a figure at a table.

It was the blind man's apartment!

"Come on in, you two!

What's the matter—scared?"

They were so scared they went in.
"There's the milk," Sam shouted.
"We didn't take it!"
"Who said you did?"
snapped the man.
"I brought it in myself.
Stop shaking, kids.
Shut the door and sit down."

Sam shut the door and sat down.

"How'd you know we're kids?" asked Ben.

"I know about you boys. You live upstairs," said the man.

"I know something else about you, Sam."

"What?" whispered Sam.

"You like the little girl across the hall. The way you slow down when you pass her door. The real nice way you say 'Hi, Betsy,' and she says 'Hi, Sam.'"

Ben giggled.

Sam jumped up.

"Who's nosy now?" he yelled. "I know about you too. You sit around here, finding out other people's secrets!" The man's face took on a faraway look.

"I know plenty, young fellow. I know when it rains, when it snows, what people are cooking, and what they think they're fighting about. Secrets? You want to hear some secrets? Listen."

He stood up suddenly, raised his harmonica
to his mouth, and began to play.
He played purples and grays and rain
and smoke and the sounds of night.
Sam sat quietly and listened.
He felt that all the sights and sounds
and colors from outside had come
into the room and were floating around.
He floated with them.
Ben's eyes were closed, and he was smiling.

After a while, Sam turned to the man and said,
"Would you like to take a walk with us tomorrow?"
The music became so soft and quiet
they could barely hear it.

Then the dark room filled with wild,
noisy, happy music.
It bounced from wall to wall.
Sam and Ben looked at each other.
They couldn't wait for tomorrow.